Dirty Bertie

ALIENS!

DAVID ROBERTS WRITTEN BY ALAN MACDONALD

Stripes

Collect all the
Dirty Bertie books!

Dirty Bertie

ALIENS!

For all the aliens out there ~ D R

To Jacob Moorhouse – and all at Gonville

School, Wanganui, New Zealand ~ A M

STRIPES PUBLISHING
An imprint of Little Tiger Press
1 The Coda Centre, 189 Munster Road,
London SW6 6AW

A paperback original
First published in Great Britain in 2015

Characters created by David Roberts
Text copyright © Alan MacDonald, 2015
Illustrations copyright © David Roberts, 2015

ISBN: 978-1-84715-512-2

Printed and bound in the UK.

10 9 8 7 6 5 4 3 2 1

Contents

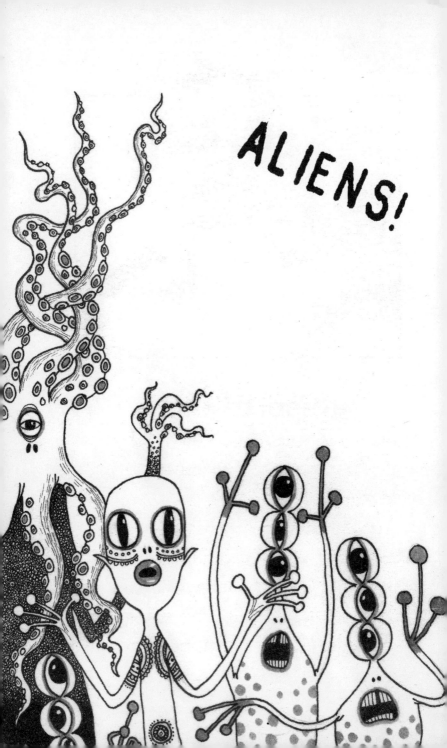

CHAPTER 1

"Race you!" said Darren on the way back from school. "Last one to the corner is a dummy!"

Bertie and Eugene chased after him. But as Bertie reached the library he skidded to a halt. A large, brightly coloured poster caught his eye. It showed a picture of a flying saucer.

ALIENS
IS ANYBODY OUT THERE?

A Talk by BARRY NUTTING
(P.U.S.S. Pudsley UFO Spotters' Society)

Bertie stared. He had never been to a talk at the library. Usually they were about flower arranging or Roman pots. But aliens? That was a different matter. Bertie had seen every alien film ever made – or at least the ones his parents had let him watch. He had an alien pencil case and a poster of the planets on his bedroom wall.

8

Dirty Bertie

"What kept you?" panted Darren, as he and Eugene came back to join him.

"Have you seen this?" asked Bertie. "Do you think aliens really exist?"

"Probably," said Darren. "Look at Know-All Nick, he's definitely an alien."

"But *real* aliens," said Bertie.

Darren shook his head. "If they exist, how come nobody's ever met one?"

"Who says they haven't?" argued Bertie. "Maybe this Nutting guy has seen one."

Eugene was still staring at the poster. "I've never seen an alien, but I've seen planets," he said.

Dirty Bertie

"When?" asked Darren.

"Lots of times," replied Eugene. "Through a telescope."

"You've got a telescope?" said Bertie, amazed.

"It's my dad's, he got it last month," said Eugene. "He keeps it in the top room."

Bertie was impressed – a real telescope!  The only telescope he owned was a plastic pirate one with a cracked lens.

"Could I have a go on it?" he asked.

Eugene hesitated. "My dad doesn't really like people touching it – apart from me," he said.

"I'm not going to break it," said Bertie. "I just want a little look."

"We could come round when your dad's not there," suggested Darren.

Eugene looked doubtful. "Maybe," he said. "I think he's out tonight, but we'd have to wait until it's dark."

"Great!" said Bertie. This was going to be brilliant. They could see the moon and comets and maybe a shooting star or two. Best of all, they might even see an actual UFO. Imagine that – a spaceship zooming towards Earth from a distant galaxy! Bertie got goosebumps just thinking about it.

CHAPTER 2

Later that evening, Eugene crept
upstairs with Bertie and Darren. His
dad was out at a meeting, but Eugene
was worried he might return and catch
them. The new telescope stood on a
tripod by a large window. Bertie gasped.
It was about twenty times the size of his
pirate telescope.

12

Dirty Bertie

"It's mega!" he said, reaching out a hand.

"Don't touch!" cried Eugene. "Dad goes crazy if there are marks on the lens. He'll know I've been using it."

"Okay, keep your wig on," said Bertie.

Eugene showed them how to look through the telescope and focus on an object. Bertie couldn't wait to have a go.

"Me first," he cried.

"That's not fair! Why you?" argued Darren.

"I'm the oldest," said Bertie.

"No you're not, I am!"

Dirty Bertie

In the end they tossed a coin and Darren won. Bertie was forced to wait impatiently, listening to Darren going on about how amazing it was.

At long last it was Bertie's turn and he squinted through the lens. At first all he could see was a fuzzy pink blob, but it turned out that he was pointing the telescope at Eugene's face. Once he tilted it upwards, the night sky came into focus. He could see brilliant stars – millions of them.

Dirty Bertie

"There's the moon!" he said. "Wow! It's like a massive cheeseball!"

Bertie moved the telescope. Stars and more stars…

"WHAT WAS THAT?" he gasped.

"What?" said Eugene.

"Something just whizzed across the sky!" said Bertie. "Like a streak of light."

"Where? Let me see!" cried Eugene.

Eugene and Darren both crowded in to look, but whatever Bertie saw had vanished.

"It was probably a shooting star," said Eugene, disappointed.

Bertie shook his head. "You know what it was?" he said dramatically. "A UFO!"

"A UFO?" snorted Darren. "You mean an alien spaceship?"

"Why not?" said Bertie. "It was going like crazy."

Darren pulled a face. "You're bonkers, Bertie," he said.

Bertie ignored him and put his eye to the telescope again. A UFO – that's *exactly* what it was! A ball of light speeding like a rocket. What if it *was* an alien spaceship? Bertie's heart beat faster. What if aliens were on their way to Earth right now and he was the only one who'd seen them?

That night Bertie dreamed that aliens had invaded his school. His whole class had turned into aliens, each with the pale, ugly face of Know-All Nick.

Bertie woke up in a cold sweat. Thank goodness it was only a dream! Then he remembered the bright streak of light he'd seen through the telescope. He sat up in bed. If it *was* a UFO, he had to tell someone. Someone who knew about aliens and would believe him.

CHAPTER 3

The next morning Bertie hurried down
to the kitchen.

"Dad, can we go to the library?" he
pleaded. "There's a talk I want to hear."

Dad raised an eyebrow. A talk? At
the library? Usually on a Saturday Bertie
met his friends at the sweet shop.
Still, a talk might be educational and it

wasn't often that Bertie begged to go to the library.

When Dad and Bertie arrived, the talk on UFOs had just begun. They sat at the back and listened as a series of pictures came up on a screen. When it was over, Bertie insisted his dad wait behind while he asked Mr Nutting something. The expert was packing away his papers.

"'Scuse me," said Bertie. "Can I ask you a question?"

"Of course. Fire away, young man," said Mr Nutting.

"Have you actually met any aliens?" asked Bertie.

"Met them? Well, no!" laughed Mr Nutting. "But that doesn't mean they don't exist. As I told you, there have been hundreds of sightings of UFOs — this one for instance."

He pointed to a photo of a blurry blob, like a fried egg in the sky. Bertie looked closer.

"That's it, *that's* what I saw!" he said excitedly.

"You?"

"Yes," said Bertie. "I was looking through a telescope last night and it zoomed across the sky!"

Mr Nutting raised his eyebrows.

"Astonishing!" he said. "Well, who knows, perhaps it *was* a UFO."

"The thing is, what do I do?" asked Bertie.

"Do?" said Mr Nutting.

"Yes – I mean if it's a spaceship and aliens have landed, how do I find them?" asked Bertie.

Mr Nutting smiled. "If I could answer that I'd be famous," he said. "The day someone makes contact with aliens will be the greatest day in history."

"REALLY?" said Bertie.

He would have liked to stay and talk, but he was in a rush to meet his friends. Taking one of Mr Nutting's leaflets, he left the library deep in thought. So it *was* an alien spaceship he'd seen – the expert had confirmed it! But where was it now? Had it landed nearby – in the woods or on the tennis courts? Either way Bertie was determined to find it. Just think,

the aliens might invite him back to their
planet to be King!

Outside the sweet shop, Darren and
Eugene were waiting.

"Where have you been?" demanded
Darren. "We've been waiting HOURS!"

"I went to the library," said Bertie. "And
listen to this – that thing I saw, it *was* a
UFO!"

Eugene bit in to a jelly snake. "How
do you know?"

"Because I asked the UFO man," said
Bertie. "He says spaceships are spotted
practically every week. So, what if one has
landed? What if the aliens are here *now*?"

"At the sweet shop?" asked Darren.

"NO! Anywhere!" said Bertie.

Darren sucked a toffee. "Listen, you're not going to meet any aliens," he sighed.

"Why not?" said Bertie.

"And even if it *was* a UFO you saw, how would you find it?" asked Eugene.

Bertie had thought of that. "I'm going to send the aliens a message," he said. "I'll send it tonight and then we'll see what happens!"

Darren nudged Eugene. "Maybe Bertie's right," he grinned. "You never know, the aliens might even answer."

Dirty Bertie

That evening, as it grew dark, Bertie stood in the back garden pointing a torch at the sky. He flashed it on and off several times to send a message to the alien visitors. Just to make sure, he spelled out a message in stones in the flower bed…

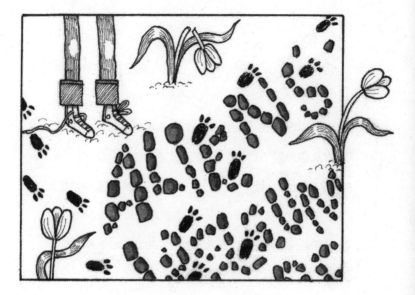

CHAPTER 4

Next morning, Bertie threw on his
clothes and hurried outside. His message
was still there but the only footprints in
the flower bed belonged to Whiffer.

Bertie trailed back inside. Surely the
aliens couldn't have missed his message?
He'd spelled it out in capital letters!
He slumped on the sofa to watch TV.

Dirty Bertie

DING DONG!

"Bertie, can you get that?" called Mum.

Bertie dragged himself off the sofa and went to open the door. *Yikes!* Was he dreaming? Standing outside were two actual aliens, large as life! They had green faces and enormous bug eyes, exactly like the aliens in films.

"FLUB!" said the taller one.

"FLOB!" said the other, waving a space gun.

Bertie was so excited he could hardly speak. The aliens had answered his message – here they were, standing at his front door!

"WHO IS IT?" called Mum.

"Um … just the postman!" Bertie shouted back.

He couldn't let his mum see the aliens. She'd probably scream the house down and scare them away.

"Come in, come in!" he whispered, beckoning to them.

Bertie hurried the aliens upstairs to his bedroom and closed the door. He had so many questions he hardly knew where to start.

"Where's your spaceship? What planet are you from?" he asked. "I'm Bertie, by the way. Ber-tie."

He pointed at himself, to make them understand.

"FLIB, FLUB, FLOB!" cried his visitors, sitting down on the bed. For aliens, they seemed pretty friendly.

"This is amazing," said Bertie. "Wait till Darren and Eugene hear about this!"

Dirty Bertie

The aliens looked at each other.
Bertie's thoughts were racing. No one
was going to believe this, not unless they
saw it with their own eyes. But who
could he tell? Bertie's eye
fell on a leaflet on the
floor. Of course! Mr
Nutting – he was
an expert on stuff
like this!

"Wait here,"
Bertie told his
visitors. "I'll bring
you something to eat."

He hurried downstairs to the phone
in the hall. Luckily Mr Nutting answered
after a moment.

"You better come quickly," said
Bertie, keeping his voice low.

"What? Who is this?" asked Mr Nutting.

"It's me, Bertie," said Bertie. "I spoke to you after your talk."

"Oh, the boy at the library," said Mr Nutting.

"Yes, but listen, I've got two aliens here – at my house!" said Bertie.

"ALIENS?" Mr Nutting snorted. "Is this your idea of a joke?"

"No, I'm serious!" replied Bertie. "I left them a message and they came."

"Look, I really don't have time for games," sighed Mr Nutting.

"Fine, don't come," said Bertie. "But if you don't, you'll be missing the greatest day in history."

There was a long silence on the other end of the phone.

"Give me your address," said Mr Nutting at last. "I'll be there in ten minutes – and this had better not be a joke!"

Bertie returned to the aliens who were fighting on the bed. They sat up when they saw he'd brought the biscuit tin.

"Chocolate biscuits," said Bertie, miming eating. "Yum yum!"

The aliens seemed to have trouble eating the biscuits, but soon they were interrupted by the doorbell.

Bertie rushed to the top of the stairs. ARGH! His mum had beaten him to it!

She opened the front door to two

large bearded men, who seemed out of breath.

"Ah, my name's Nutting, pleased to meet you," said the UFO expert. "This is my friend Mr Potts. Your son called me."

"Bertie?" said Mum.

"Yes, is it true?" said Mr Nutting. "I thought he was making it up, but I had to see for myself. Are they upstairs?"

Dad came out of the lounge. "What's all this about?" he asked, puzzled.

"Well … the aliens!" said Mr Nutting. "Didn't Bertie tell you?"

Dad rolled his eyes. He might have known all this talk of UFOs would go to Bertie's head. Now Bertie was imagining little green men.

"BERTIE!" he yelled. "GET DOWN HERE!"

Dirty Bertie

Bertie crept slowly downstairs.

Mum folded her arms. "Aliens?" she said. "I'm told we have some in the house?"

"Mmm," said Bertie, nodding. "I um … suppose you want to see them?"

"I think we'd better, don't you?" said Mum.

Bertie disappeared. A minute later he was back with two small bug-eyed creatures.

Dirty Bertie

Mr Nutting let out a groan. "That's them? The aliens?"

"Yes," said Bertie. "They just turned up at the house."

"Did they?" said Mum. "I think I can guess why."

She pulled off the aliens' rubber masks. Darren and Eugene grinned.

"FLOB!" said Eugene.

"FLIB!" said Darren. "HA! HA! Fooled you, Bertie!"

Bertie looked stunned. How could he have been so stupid? He should have guessed it was his friends playing a trick.

Mum, Dad and the UFO spotters glared at him, waiting for an explanation.

Bertie threw up his hands helplessly. "Well, anyone can make a mistake!"

TWITTER!

CHAPTER 1

Bertie and his friends came out of the school gates. It was Friday and he was looking forward to a whole weekend without Miss Boot shouting in his ear.

"Guess what I'm doing tomorrow," said Eugene. "Birdwatching with Dad!"

Bertie raised his eyebrows. "Birdwatching?"

Dirty Bertie

"Bor-ing!" sang Darren.

"It's not!" said Eugene. "Last time we went it was the best day ever – we saw a spotted woodpecker! You have to stay really, really quiet."

"It sounds like school," said Bertie.

Eugene ignored him. "Anyway, Dad says I can bring a friend tomorrow," he went on. "So what do you think?"

Bertie looked at Darren. "US? Go *birdwatching*?" he said.

"Yes!" said Eugene. "Well, only one of you. Dad says three's too many."

Darren shook his head. "It's okay, you go, Bertie," he grinned. "I've got football practice."

"That's not fair!" grumbled Bertie. "Why do *I* have to go?"

Eugene looked hurt. "It'll be brilliant!"

he said. "Just think, a whole day out in the woods."

Bertie couldn't see what was so brilliant about it. If he wanted to watch birds he could do it from his bedroom window. In any case, birds just hopped about pecking and twittering – they didn't really *do* anything. If they had to *watch* something, what about lions or crocodiles?

"Couldn't we go to the zoo instead?" suggested Bertie.

"No, it's all arranged now," sighed Eugene. "I thought you'd *want* to come."

"He *does* want to come, don't you, Bertie?" sniggered Darren.

"Of course I do," said Bertie. "It's just ... well, what would we *do* all day?"

Dirty Bertie

"There's loads to do in a wood,"
said Eugene.

This was true, thought Bertie. At
least there would be trees to climb and
branches to swing from. They could
hunt for slimy slugs or wriggly worms
and take a few home.

"So we can run off and play?" asked Bertie.

"Maybe," said Eugene. "As long as we don't make a noise."

Bertie shrugged. "Okay, I'll think about it," he said.

Back home, Bertie helped himself to orange juice from the fridge. His mum came into the kitchen.

"Oh, Bertie, what are you up to tomorrow?" she asked.

"I don't know yet," said Bertie. "Why?"

"Because Angela's coming round to play," replied Mum.

"ANGELA?" Bertie choked so hard that orange juice spurted out of his nose.

How could his mum do this to him?
Angela Nicely lived next door and she
was always begging to come round.
She'd probably want to play dollies' tea
parties or something. He needed to find
an excuse, and fast. But wait, he already
had one…

"Oh *tomorrow*?" he said. "I'm going
birdwatching with Eugene tomorrow."

Dirty Bertie

"Birdwatching?" said Mum. "Since when were you interested in birds?"

"Birds are very interesting actually," Bertie informed her. "If you're quiet you can see a spotty wormpecker or something."

"You mean a woodpecker," said Mum. "But can't you go another day?"

Bertie shook his head. "Sorry, it's all arranged. Eugene's dad's taking us."

Mum sighed heavily. "Very well, I'll have to put Angela off," she said. "I'm sure she'll be really disappointed."

Bertie breathed out. That was close. Even birdwatching was better than a whole day with awful Angela!

CHAPTER 2

Early the next morning, Eugene and his dad came to collect Bertie for the trip.

"Now I want you to be on your best behaviour," warned Mum. "Don't go running off."

"I won't," said Bertie.

"And no fighting or rolling in the mud," said Mum.

"I won't," said Bertie.

"And remember your please and thankyous," said Mum. "Be polite to Mr Clark."

"I won't," said Bertie, who wasn't really listening. Honestly, the way his mum went on, you would think he was meeting the Prime Minister.

He climbed into the back of the car beside Eugene and they set off.

"Well?" said Mr Clark. "I hope you're as excited as Eugene."

"Um … yes, I can't wait," replied Bertie.

"Bertie's never been birdwatching before," explained Eugene.

"*Really?*" said Mr Clark, as if this was astonishing news. "Well, you're in for a treat. Last time we saw a chiffchaff and two nuthatches, didn't we, Eugene?"

Dirty Bertie

"Yes," said Eugene. "And don't forget the woodpecker!"

"Show Bertie the book I got you," said Mr Clark.

Eugene pulled out a book from his rucksack. It was called *The Little Bird Spotter's Guide*.

Bertie turned the pages. He never knew there were so many birds! There were millions of them – big, small, speckled, long-legged, beaky and beady-eyed.

Dirty Bertie

Bertie pointed to the picture of a bird with a sharp, hooked beak.

"Wow! This one looks mean!" he said.

"That's a hawk, they're birds of prey," said Eugene. "They swoop down and catch mice and stuff. Sometimes they even carry off other birds."

Bertie's eyes widened. This sounded more like it. He wouldn't mind spotting a mean killer hawk!

"Will we see one today?" he asked.

"I doubt it!" laughed Mr Clark. "You don't get many hawks in Fernley Woods. Anyway, we're looking for something else."

"The marsh warbler," said Eugene, nodding.

"They're pretty rare, but one was sighted recently," said his dad. "If we're very quiet and really patient we might just get lucky."

Eugene showed Bertie a picture of the marsh warbler. It was a fat little greeny-brown bird with a white chest. Bertie hardly glanced at it. He'd much rather see a killer hawk swooping down from the sky. One day he was going to get a pet hawk and train it to attack his enemies. Imagine Miss Boot's face when she was suddenly carried off in the middle of assembly.

CHAPTER 3

PLOP, PLOP, PLOP!

The rain pitter-pattered on the roof of the bird hide. Bertie passed the binoculars back to Eugene. They'd been watching the woods for HOURS, but all they'd seen was trees, bushes and pouring rain.

The hide was a bit like a garden shed

only bigger and colder. There were
hard benches to sit on and long narrow
windows to look out of. Eugene's dad
said that the idea was to stay hidden so
they wouldn't frighten the birds away.
Not that there *were* any birds. Bertie
was beginning to think they'd all gone on
holiday.

"See anything?" asked Mr Clark.

Eugene shook his head.

"Wait, there *is* something!" he
whispered. "Look – under the tree!"

His dad peered through the
binoculars.

"Ah yes, it's a sparrow," he said.
"Never mind."

Even Bertie knew that sparrows were
not rare birds.

"How much longer?" he groaned.

Dirty Bertie

Mr Clark shot him a look.

"You must learn to be patient, Bertie," he said. "It's all about keeping your eyes open."

"Can't we have lunch?" moaned Bertie.

"We just got here! It's only eleven o'clock," said Mr Clark.

"But I'm STARVING!" cried Bertie.

Mr Clark shook his head. It was nice for Eugene to bring a friend, but he was starting to wish it wasn't Bertie. The boy had no interest in nature at all. Worse still, he never stopped talking, fidgeting or picking his nose.

Mr Clark dug into his bag and brought out a strange-looking whistle.

"I thought I might try this – it's a bird-caller," he explained. "It attracts

birds because they think they hear
another bird calling."

He raised the bird-
caller to his lips and
blew gently.

"*Throop-oo! Throop-oo!*"

"Amazing!" said Eugene.
"It sounds just like a bird!"

"Can I have a go?" asked
Bertie.

"Er … maybe it's better if I do it," said
Eugene's dad.

"*Pleeeeease!* Just one little go," begged
Bertie. "I'm not going to break it!"

Mr Clark smiled weakly and handed
him the bird-caller. Bertie thought it
might attract a passing hawk, looking for
mice or weasels. He stood on the bench
and blew a deafening blast.

"THROOP-
OOO! THROOP-
OOOOO!"

"Okay, that's
enough now," said
Mr Clark hastily.

But Bertie didn't stop.

"THROOP-OO! THROOP-OO!
THROOP— URGH!"

Mr Clark snatched the bird-caller from
his mouth.

"I said that's enough!" he snapped.
"You'll scare every bird in the wood.
Now *please* sit still and keep quiet!"

Bertie slumped on to the bench. He
was only trying to help – you'd think
that Eugene's dad would be grateful!
He picked up an empty plastic cup
and put it between his teeth.

"What am I?" he asked Eugene.

"Dunno," laughed Eugene. "A nutcase."

"A HAWK!" cried Bertie.

He flapped his arms and swooped down upon Eugene. They both fell off the bench and rolled on the floor, giggling.

Dirty Bertie

"For the last time, STOP IT!" yelled Mr Clark, losing patience. "Eugene, I'm surprised at you. Do you want to see a marsh warbler or not?"

Eugene got up. "Sorry, Dad," he mumbled.

Bertie sighed heavily. He wished the stupid bird would turn up soon, then they could all go home!

CHAPTER 4

Bertie jiggled his legs. He'd drunk all his lemonade and now he was desperate for the loo, but Eugene's dad wanted them to keep watch in silence.

"'Scuse me!" whispered Bertie.

"SHHH!" hissed Mr Clark.

"I can't shhh!" moaned Bertie. "I need the toilet!"

Dirty Bertie

"There isn't one," said Mr Clark.

"Go in the woods, that's what I always do," suggested Eugene.

"Fine," said his dad. "But don't go far and DON'T make any noise!"

Bertie hurried to the door. It was no wonder that not many children went birdwatching, he thought. If they added a café, toilets and maybe a zip wire then more people might come.

He ducked out of the hide and looked around for somewhere to go. There was a rough path leading off into the woods. Bertie followed it, half walking and half running. It wasn't easy to hurry quietly.

At last he reached a muddy bank by a pool of water. There were plenty of trees around and no one about.

Bertie closed his eyes and let out
a long sigh of relief. Then he heard
something — singing.

A fat little bird with a white front
sat on a branch twittering away. Bertie
watched it hop down to the water's
edge. He dug in his pocket and found a
few crisps that he'd been saving for later.
He scattered them on the ground.

"Here, birdy birdy!" he called softly.
"Look – crisps!"

The fat little bird hopped closer until
it was only a few steps away. Bertie
kept as still as a statue. Finally the bird
pecked at a crisp.

Bertie watched it for a minute or
two. It was quite a nice bird, even if it
wasn't a killer hawk. Finally it flew away,
vanishing into the treetops.

"Bye-bye, birdy!" called Bertie, with a wave.

Back at the hide, Bertie crept in the door. Eugene and his dad hadn't moved from their posts.

"Better?" whispered Eugene.

"Yes thanks," said Bertie. "There's loads of trees we could climb, and guess what – I saw a bird!"

"What kind of bird?" asked Eugene.

"Dunno, just a small one," replied Bertie.

"Probably a sparrow," said Eugene.

"No, this was fatter," said Bertie. "Sort of a greeny-brown colour."

Mr Clark looked at him, gripping his binoculars.

"What colour chest did it have?" he demanded.

"White, I think," said Bertie. "It was singing."

Mr Clark turned pale. He grabbed *The Little Bird Spotter's Guide* and turned the pages.

"Think! Was it anything like this?" he asked, pointing to a picture.

"YES!" cried Bertie. "That's the one! That's it exactly!"

Mr Clark closed his eyes. "A marsh warbler!" he moaned. "You saw a marsh warbler. YOU!"

"That's good then," said Bertie. "It ate my crisps."

Bertie thought Mr Clark would have been pleased, but he didn't look it. He paced up and down, waving his hands in the air.

"UNBELIEVABLE!" he fumed. "You talk, you fidget, you blunder off into the woods and what happens? You see a marsh warbler. You, of all people!"

"Anyway," said Bertie. "Now I've seen it, can we go home?"

Mr Clark insisted they return to the spot where Bertie had seen the rare bird. They waited for another hour, but the marsh warbler didn't come back.

Mr Clark drove them home in silence. He seemed to be sulking. Bertie couldn't see what he was so cross about. After all, it wasn't *his* fault that no one else saw the marsh warbler! Besides, it was only a bird! If he'd seen a crocodile, *that* would have been something to get excited about.

Dirty Bertie

Back home, Mum let him in and made him take off his muddy boots in the hall.

"So how was birdwatching?" she asked.

Bertie shrugged. "Okay," he sighed. "But it'd be better if they had slides or a zip wire."

"I hope you behaved yourself," said Mum.

"Of course," said Bertie. "I hardly said a word all day!"

In any case, he didn't think he'd be invited to go again, which was probably just as well.

Better still, he had avoided a whole

day of Angela Nicely. That would have been torture! And there was still an hour to watch TV before suppertime. He opened the lounge door.

"HI, BERTIE!" sang a voice that made his heart sink. "Your mum said I could come for supper! Isn't that nice?"

Bertie groaned. NOT ANGELA! Life was so unfair!

CHAPTER 1

Bertie was on his way home from
school with Darren and Eugene. He
took out a large brown envelope
from his bag and stared at it for the
hundredth time. Inside was the thing he
dreaded every year – his school report.
He hadn't read it yet because mean old
Miss Boot had sealed the envelope.

Dirty Bertie

Why do teachers have to write reports anyway? thought Bertie. *Why don't children write reports on their teachers? That would be much fairer!* He knew exactly what he'd say…

> Miss Boot is the wurst teacher in the univers. She is bad tempered, grouchy and canot spell for tofee.

Eugene shook his head. "There's no point staring at it," he said.

"I just want to *know*," grumbled Bertie. "It's *my* report so why can't I see it?"

"Because you're not allowed," replied Eugene. "Miss Boot said we have to give it to our parents."

Dirty Bertie

Darren raised an eyebrow. "But Miss Boot's not here, is she?" he said.

Bertie looked round to check their teacher wasn't hiding behind a lamp post. You could never be too sure. He fingered the envelope.

"Shall I?" he asked.

"Go on," said Darren. "Let's all open them together!"

"We can't!" moaned Eugene. "We'll get in trouble!"

"Not if we're careful," said Bertie. "If we stick the envelope back down, who's going to know?"

Eugene looked worried, but he was dying to see his report just like the others.

Very carefully, Bertie unsealed his envelope, taking care not to tear it.

Dirty Bertie

He took a deep breath and pulled out his report. Miss Boot's spidery handwriting filled the page…

The others opened their reports.

"Phew!" said Eugene. "Mine's pretty good! It says 'Eugene is very hard-working'."

"And mine's not so bad," said Darren. "What about you, Bertie?"

Bertie looked up. "Terrible!" he groaned. "Listen to this: 'Bertie is messy, idle and never listens. If anything, his work has gone backwards this year, which is quite an achievement!'"

Darren laughed. "You *always* get a bad report," he said.

"It's not funny!" said Bertie. "The last one was so terrible I had to promise my mum that I'd improve this year. Otherwise she's going to find me a tutor!"

"A *tutor?*" repeated Darren.

"You mean, like your own teacher?" said Eugene.

"Exactly!" said Bertie.

It was bad enough seeing teachers at school without one turning up at your house. There'd be no more TV, going to the park or having fun. His life would just be work, work, work from morning till night.

No, thought Bertie, it was too horrible to imagine. He had to make sure his parents never set eyes on the report. But how? As soon as he got home, his mum would want to read it.

Bertie frowned. Wait a moment – what if his report never reached home? What if he accidentally lost it? He looked around and spotted a red postbox up ahead. Perfect! If he posted the report he'd never see it again – it would be gone forever!

He slipped the report back in the envelope and marched up to the postbox.

"What are you doing?" asked Eugene.

"I'm posting it," replied Bertie.

Dirty Bertie

"YOU CAN'T DO THAT!" cried Eugene.

"Why can't I?" said Bertie.

Before they could stop him, he pushed the envelope into the slot…

FLUMP!

It disappeared.

"Bye-bye, report!" said Bertie, patting the postbox on the head.

CHAPTER 2

Darren shook his head. "You nutter!" he laughed. "What did you do that for?"

"Miss Boot's going to kill you!" said Eugene.

"She'll never find out," said Bertie. "My address isn't even on the envelope."

"But what about your mum and dad?" asked Eugene. "They'll be expecting it."

Dirty Bertie

"No they won't," argued Bertie. "They don't even know we've got our reports."

"They'll find out when they go to Parents' Evening," said Darren.

Bertie stared. "To… What?"

"Parents' Evening," repeated Darren. "It's this Friday, remember?"

Bertie's legs turned to jelly. How could he have forgotten Parents' Evening? Miss Boot had gone on and on about it when she was handing out their reports. It was on Friday – the day after tomorrow!

"Miss Boot always talks about our reports with our parents," said Eugene. "That's what Parents' Evening is for."

"Yeah, so how are you going to explain that yours has disappeared?" asked Darren.

Bertie looked at the postbox in

horror. ARGH! What had he done? He had to get his report back or he was in serious trouble!

He peered into the mouth of the postbox.

"It's too late now," said Darren. "You'll never get it back."

Bertie wasn't listening. He squeezed his hand through the hole and felt around.

"I can't reach it!" he wailed.

"You've got no chance," said Eugene. "Just leave it!" But Bertie wasn't giving up that easily. He wriggled his arm in up to the elbow and fished around inside. It was no use.

78

Dirty Bertie

"Well, don't just stand there!" he grumbled. "Help me!"

"HEY YOU! GET AWAY FROM THERE!"

Bertie looked round. Yikes! It was the postman! He was getting out of his van and coming towards them. Bertie yanked his arm free so quickly that he almost fell flat on his back.

The postman set down his sack and glared.

"What do you think you're doing?" he demanded.

"Sorry," mumbled Bertie. "I lost my report."

"Your what?"

"My report, from school," explained Bertie. "I sort of, um … accidentally posted it."

The postman stared.

"You *accidentally* posted it?"

Bertie nodded. "Yes, it was a mistake, but now I need it back."

Dirty Bertie

The postman shook his head and took out a bunch of keys to unlock the postbox.

"Well, it's too late now," he said, opening his sack.

"But can't you look for it?" pleaded Bertie. "It's in a big brown envelope."

"There are hundreds of envelopes, and once they're in the box I've got to collect them," said the postman. "I can't go rummaging around."

Bertie watched helplessly as the pile of letters disappeared into the sack.

POST

"Please!" he begged. "If I don't get it back, Miss Boot will kill me."

"You should have thought of that before," said the postman. "Now I've got to get on. And in future, keep your hands out of the postbox."

He dumped the sack into the back of his van, slammed the door and drove off. Bertie watched the van disappear along with his last hope. He was done for. What on earth was he going to do?

CHAPTER 3

Back home, Bertie tried to slip in quietly and sneak upstairs.

"BERTIE? Is that you?" called Mum from the lounge.

"Um … it might be," replied Bertie.

Mum appeared in the doorway. "What are you up to?" she asked. Bertie wasn't usually quiet when he came in.

"Nothing!" said Bertie. "I'm just going to get changed."

"Well, there are clean clothes on your bed," said Mum. "But save them for Friday – it's your Parents' Evening."

Bertie groaned. He was hoping his mum might have forgotten, but no such luck. Any minute now she'd probably ask if he'd got his school report. If only he could borrow one – Know-All Nick's for instance. He *always* got a glowing report.

Suddenly Bertie's face lit up with an idea. What if he wrote his *own* report? Then he could have the report he deserved.

Bertie has amazed evrywon this yeer. be is a shyning eggsample to his klass – and speshlly to that fat head No-All Nick. ★ ★ ★

Dirty Bertie

Ten minutes later Bertie came downstairs, holding a large envelope in his hand.

"What's that?" asked Mum.

"This? It's my report," said Bertie. "Miss Boot gave them out today."

Mum took the envelope. "Well, I hope it's a lot better than your last one," she said grimly. "You remember what I told you?"

Bertie remembered only too well. Mum studied the report and frowned at him.

"Miss Boot wrote this?" she said.

Bertie nodded. "Um … yes, is it all right?"

"It's more than all right," said Mum. "Miss Boot is singing your praises."

"Is she?" said Bertie. "I guess it must be cos I've been working hard and paying attention and stuff."

"Have you now?" said Mum, narrowing her eyes.

Dad came into the lounge.

"Bertie's got his report," Mum told him.

"Oh yes?" said Dad. "What's it like?"

"Well, Miss Boot claims that he is 'dead clever' and 'top of the class'," said Mum.

Dad looked astonished. "*Seriously?*" he said, taking the report.

Bertie didn't see why everyone sounded so shocked. He'd have thought they would be delighted with his progress. Dad was reading the report for himself.

Dirty Bertie

"Class is spelt with a 'K'," he said.

"Yes," said Mum. "And I can hardly read Miss Boot's handwriting. You would *almost* say it was as bad as Bertie's writing."

"Hmm, funny that," said Dad, raising his eyebrows.

Mum folded her arms. "Well, I shall look forward to discussing this report with Miss Boot," she said.

Dirty Bertie

Bertie almost choked. Miss Boot? If she saw the report she'd guess who had written it in three seconds. Worse still, she'd want to know what had happened to the REAL report.

"Oh … um … didn't I say?" spluttered Bertie. "Miss Boot said she can't come to Parents' Evening."

"Can't come? Why not?" demanded Mum.

"Because she's … she's sick," said Bertie, thinking quickly. "She lost her voice from shouting at Darren so much."

"When did this happen?" asked Dad.

"Today!" said Bertie. "She was shouting, then suddenly her voice went and she said she can't come to Parents' Evening."

"I see," said Mum. "And how did she tell you that if she'd lost her voice?"

Dirty Bertie

Bertie gulped. "She um … she wrote it on the board," he said.

Mum and Dad exchanged looks.

"Well, I'm sure the school will let us know," said Mum. "I think we'll take a chance and go along anyway."

"NO!" squawked Bertie. "I mean … you'd just be wasting your time."

Mum gave him a long hard look. "We are going, whether you like it or not, Bertie," she said. "Anyone would think you had something to hide."

CHAPTER 4

Friday came round all too soon.
Bertie found himself sitting outside his
classroom, watching the clock tick by.
He had been to the toilet three times
already. He could hear Miss Boot's voice
booming like distant thunder. Know-All
Nick was in there with his parents. Bertie
was next on the list.

Dirty Bertie

"Well, it sounds like Miss Boot's got her voice back," said Dad.

"Mmm," said Bertie faintly. "Actually I feel a bit sick. Maybe I should lie down?"

"You'll live," said Mum. "Our appointment's in five minutes."

Bertie glanced down at the report poking out of his mum's bag. As soon as Miss Boot saw it he would be dead meat.

Just then the classroom door opened. Know-All Nick appeared with his parents. Nick's mum saw Bertie's mum and smiled.

Dirty Bertie

"I *do* enjoy these Parents' Evenings, don't you?" she trilled. "Such a pleasure to hear how *well* Nicholas is doing."

"Yes," replied Bertie's mum. "We can't wait to discuss Bertie's report."

Nick glowed with pride. "Miss Boot says I'm her star pupil," he boasted. "What did your report say, Bertie?"

"Mind your own business," Bertie replied.

"Never mind," jeered Nick. "Someone has to come bottom of the class. HAW HAW HAW!"

"For your information, I wasn't bottom, I came top," said Bertie.

"LIAR!" snorted Nick. "I *always* come top."

Dirty Bertie

"Not this time, smarty pants," said Bertie.

"We'll see about that," said Nick. "You better not keep Miss Boot waiting! I'm sure she's got *lots* to tell you."

Bertie breathed in. This was it. There was no escape. He followed his mum and dad into the classroom.

Miss Boot sat waiting at her desk with her mark book open.

"Ah, do come in and take a seat!" she smiled. "I've been looking forward to this."

Dirty Bertie

Bertie sat down beside his parents. His hands were sweating. He tried not to look at his teacher.

"So I take it you didn't receive Bertie's report?" said Miss Boot.

"Oh yes, we got it all right," said Mum.

"You did?" Miss Boot sounded surprised.

"Well, he gave us *a* report," said Mum. "This one."

She took out the fake report from her bag and handed it over. Miss Boot read it and her eyebrows hit the ceiling. She read out her teacher's comment:

Bertie is ded clever. This year he woz easy top of the klass.

Bertie turned red as Miss Boot fixed him with a glare. "You wrote this drivel, did you, Bertie?" she said.

"M-me?" mumbled Bertie.

"Yes, YOU!" snapped Miss Boot.

"Did you really think you had us fooled for even a minute?" asked Dad.

Bertie shook his head dumbly.

"So where is your actual report?" asked Mum.

"Oh, I can answer that," smiled Miss Boot, reaching for a brown envelope. "Fortunately your report has turned up safe and sound."

Bertie went pale. *What?* It couldn't have! He'd seen the postman put it in his sack!

"It seems someone posted it," Miss Boot went on. "But the Post Office recognized the school's name and sent it back. Wasn't that a stroke of luck, Bertie?"

Dirty Bertie

Bertie slid down lower in his seat. It was so unfair! They could have sent the report anywhere – India, Australia, the North Pole – anywhere but back to his school!

Miss Boot leaned forward and smiled cruelly. "Now," she said. "Would you like to hear what *I* wrote about Bertie?"